The SILLY SOLAR SYSTEM

A Poetic Odyssey by Kevin Price
Illustrated by Robin Carter

The Silly Solar System

For Andrea and Albert – KP
In memory of my dear mother, Mary Carter – RC

The author would like to thank Chris Knight, Kieran O'Herlihy
and Steve Ibbotson for their help in producing this book.

Published by KAMA Publishing
19A The Swale, Norwich, NR5 9HE
www.kamapublishing.co.uk

First printed 2011
Second Edition 2012

Text © Kevin Price, 2011
Illustrations © Robin Carter

Hardback ISBN 9780956719614
Paperback ISBN 9780956719621

Printed in Great Britain by
Barnwell Print Ltd, Dunkirk, Aylsham, Norfolk. NR11 6SU

WORLD
LAND
TRUST™
www.carbonbalancedpaper.com
CBP0004121705121654

By using Carbon Balanced Paper
through the World Land Trust on this
publication we have saved 1471kg of
Carbon & preserved 123sqm of
critically threatened tropical forests.

Carbon Balanced Paper. One of the most sustainable forms of communication that
will reduce your carbon foot print and promote CSR. www.carbonbalancepaper.com

The Silly Solar System – Contents

The Silly Solar System

The famous astronomer, Patrick McFuddy,

Was using the telescope kept in his study,

When Jacob, his son, came in, clutching a book.

"What's that?" queried Patrick, "Can I take a look?"

"*It's my homework about Roman gods,*" Jacob said,

But I'd rather be learning about Space instead."

Patrick thought for a moment and then said, "Come here.

Look up through my telescope at this glowing sphere."

"*What star is that Daddy? Please tell me its name.*"

"It's known as 'The Evening Star' – let's play a game.

Space has some wonders which always enthral

And 'The Evening Star' isn't a real star at all.

I've thought of a way I can teach you some stuff –

It will help with your homework, which won't seem so tough!

Sit down in that chair," Patrick said with a grin.

"When you're sitting comfortably, then we'll begin."

The SUN

Our Solar System's a wonderful place,

A collection of planets rotating through space,

With the Sun at its heart, its own glowing star –

It's so far away we can't reach it by car.

If we want to visit, then here's what we'll need,

A spaceship which moves at incredible speed!

Imagine we've built one of just the right kind,

Blast off from the centre and what will we find?

SUN FACT BOX

Type of star	Yellow Dwarf
Mean distance to Earth	150 million km (93 million miles)
Age	4,600 million years
Diameter	1,390,000 km (870,000 miles): 110 Earths would fit across the diameter of The Sun
Composition	Hydrogen 71%, Helium 26.5%, Other 2.5%
Effective Surface Temperature	6,000° Centigrade (10,832° Fahrenheit)
Core Temperature	15 million° Centigrade (27 million° Fahrenheit)
Did you know?	The process of converting Hydrogen to Helium reduces the weight of The Sun by 4 million tonnes EVERY SECOND. This is known as the 'Mass Defect'

Mercury

57.8 million km ▶

MERCURY FACT BOX

Diameter	4,878 km (3,050 miles)
Average distance from The Sun	57.8 million km (36.125 million miles)
Diameter compared to Earth	0.4 x
Gravity compared to Earth	0.38 x
Surface temperature	Day side Max. 467° Centigrade (872° Fahrenheit). Night side Min. -183° Centigrade (-297° Fahrenheit)
Length of a day	58 Earth days and 16 hours
Length of a year	87.9 Earth days
Atmosphere Composition	Oxygen 56%, Sodium 35%, Helium 8%, Potassium & Hydrogen 1%
Did you know?	The daytime temperature on Mercury is hot enough to melt lead

Now we're on our way, what's the first thing we see?

A small, hostile planet, that's called Mercury.

Mercury's orbit is close to the Sun

And now that we've got here it isn't much fun!

Its dry, rocky surface gets mightily hot,

You may wish to land there – I'm sure we should not!

Although we'd be able to say that we'd tried,

In no time at all we'd be frizzled and fried!

That's if we landed there during the day,

The nights are so cold we would freeze straight away!

To orbit the Sun it takes eighty eight days

And it wibbles and wobbles in curious ways.

With its pits and its craters, it looks like our Moon,

But as it's so hot let's get out of here soon!

The wings on his helmet might seem a bit odd,

But the Romans knew him as 'The Messenger God'.

Venus

VENUS FACT BOX

Diameter	12,104km (7,521 miles)
Average distance from The Sun	108.2 million km (67.23 million miles)
Diameter compared to Earth	0.95x
Gravity compared to Earth	0.88x
Surface temperature	484° Centigrade (903.2° Fahrenheit)
Length of a day	243 Earth days (retrograde)
Length of a year	224.7 Earth days
Atmosphere Composition	Carbon Dioxide 96%, Nitrogen 3.5%, Sulphur Dioxide, Argon & Carbon Monoxide 0.5%
Did you know?	As Venus is permanently cloaked in dense clouds, no-one has ever seen its surface directly from Earth

108.2 million km

Next out is Venus and that's just as bad,

In poisonous cloudlets of acid it's clad!

These are so thick that you can't see right through

And they glow with an orange and yellowish hue.

If we fly through these clouds we should go at full pelt

As the acid is hot and our spaceship might melt.

We could try to land there, but if we did that,

The dense atmosphere might squash us quite flat!

And even at night we're unlikely to freeze;

The temperature's over four hundred degrees!

'The Evening Star' brightens the skies up above

And the Romans called Venus 'The Goddess of Love'.

Earth

A little bit further, we've come to the Earth,

To all sorts of life-forms the Earth's given birth.

The first creatures formed in primordial stew;

Three billion years later and here's me and you!

If we were to land there then we'd be relieved

That we'd got to a planet with air we can breathe.

Earth's the first planet that has its own Moon –

Don't worry, you'll see plenty more of them soon.

When seen from our spaceship the Earth is deep blue –

Just look through the window, you'll see that it's true!

When you're on your travels, wherever you roam,

Please always remember that Earth is your home.

149.6 million km

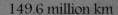

EARTH FACT BOX

Diameter	12,756 km (7,926 miles)
Average distance from The Sun	149.6 million km (92.96 million miles)
Surface temperature	From – 70° Centigrade (– 94° Fahrenheit)
	to + 55° Centigrade (+ 131° Fahrenheit)
Length of a day	23.93 hours (over 23 hours, 59 minutes)
Length of a year	365.26 days
Satellites	One – The Moon
Atmosphere Composition	Nitrogen 78%, Oxygen 21% , Other 1%
Did you know?	Earth is the only place in the entire
	Universe known to support life

EARTH'S MOON FACT BOX

Diameter	3,474 km (2,159 miles)
Average distance from Earth	384,400 km (250,000 miles)
Diameter compared to Earth	0.27x
Mean surface temperature	Day 107°C (225°F),
	Night –153°C (–243°F)
Did you know?	Without the effect of the Moon's gravity
	there would be no tides in the Earth's oceans

Ceres was the Roman goddess of Earth and
fertility. However, she had other duties too.
Look out for her later in the story.

13

Mars

228 million km

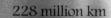

We've moved on to Mars and its colour of red,

A haven to little green men it is said.

The Victorians thought that canals crossed its plain;

That's a silly idea! It's completely insane!

The thing is you see, you just have to be told,

That nothing could live here, it's simply too cold!

Onc mountain – Olympus Mons – is so tall,

It makes the Earth's biggest – Mount Everest – look small.

There are two tiny moons, of which neither is round,

And no little green man has ever been found!

It's the scariest planet that you ever saw,

The Romans knew Mars as 'The God of War'!

MARS FACT BOX

Diameter	6,786 km (4,216 miles)
Average distance from The Sun	228 million km (141.67 million miles)
Diameter compared to Earth	0.5x
Gravity compared to Earth	0.38x
Surface temperature	Daytime Maximum 25° Centigrade (77° Fahrenheit), Nighttime Mean – 120° Centigrade (– 184° Fahrenheit)
Length of a day	24.62 Earth hours
Length of a year	687 Earth days
Satellites	Two – Phobos and Deimos
Atmosphere Composition	Carbon Dioxide 96%, Nitrogen 2.7%, Argon 1.6%, Other 0.7%
Did you know?	Olympus Mons is c. 25km (15.5 miles) high compared to Mount Everest, which is only 8.85km (5.5 miles) high

The Asteroid Belt

Now we've left Mars and gone into the void,

We're passing through thick belts of Asteroids.

These are millions of rocks of irregular size,

But what are they doing here? Why the surprise?

It's thought that a planet was meant to form here.

Would it have been blessed with a fine atmosphere?

It might have been purple, with yellows and greens,

Instead, all we're left with is these smithereens.

But hold on, what's this? Wow, look what we've found!

A rock which is larger and totally round.

An object so big it was given a name;

Its title is Ceres – what's her claim to fame?

She nurtures the wheat on the prairies and plains;

The Romans named Ceres 'The Goddess of Grain'.

415 million km

CERES FACT BOX

Diameter	950 km (590 miles)
Average distance from The Sun	415 million km (258 million miles)
Diameter compared to Earth	0.075x
Gravity compared to Earth	0.03x
Mean surface temperature	−100°C (−148°F)
Length of a day	c. 9 Earth hours
Length of a year	4.6 Earth years
Satellites	None
Atmosphere Composition	Unknown
Did you know?	Ceres is sometimes termed the first 'dwarf' planet in the Solar System

Jupiter

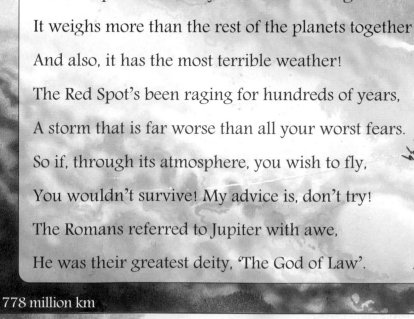

On leaving the Asteroid Belt far behind,

Go full speed ahead and then what will we find?

A planet named Jupiter, that's what we've got,

Complete with its fabulous Great Red Spot.

When planets are rated according to size,

Then Jupiter certainly wins the first prize!

Its make–up is almost entirely gas

And so, for its size, it has very low mass.

But if you are tempted to think that it's light,

I have to point out that you wouldn't be right.

It weighs more than the rest of the planets together

And also, it has the most terrible weather!

The Red Spot's been raging for hundreds of years,

A storm that is far worse than all your worst fears.

So if, through its atmosphere, you wish to fly,

You wouldn't survive! My advice is, don't try!

The Romans referred to Jupiter with awe,

He was their greatest deity, 'The God of Law'.

778 million km

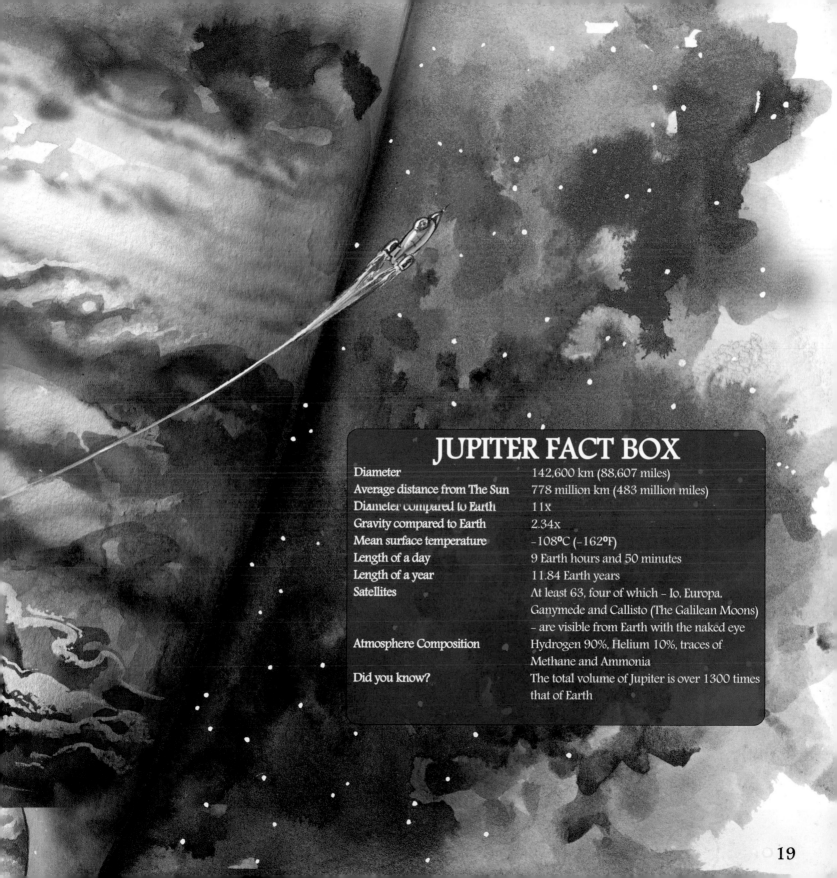

JUPITER FACT BOX

Diameter	142,600 km (88,607 miles)
Average distance from The Sun	778 million km (483 million miles)
Diameter compared to Earth	11x
Gravity compared to Earth	2.34x
Mean surface temperature	–108ºC (–162ºF)
Length of a day	9 Earth hours and 50 minutes
Length of a year	11.84 Earth years
Satellites	At least 63, four of which – Io, Europa, Ganymede and Callisto (The Galilean Moons) – are visible from Earth with the naked eye
Atmosphere Composition	Hydrogen 90%, Helium 10%, traces of Methane and Ammonia
Did you know?	The total volume of Jupiter is over 1300 times that of Earth

Jupiter's Moons

Remember we hoped there'd be more moons to see?

In Jupiter's grip, there's at least sixty three!

The four largest moons were discovered back when

Galileo first saw them in 1610.

Impressive in size and with notable girth,

These Jupiter moons can be seen from the Earth.

CALLISTO FACT BOX

Diameter	4,820 km (2,995 miles)
Average distance from Jupiter	1,882,700 km (1,169,855 miles)
Diameter compared to Earth	0.38x
Mean surface temperature	–172°C (–279°F)
Did you know?	Callisto is one of the most heavily cratered satellites in the Solar System

778 million km

IO FACT BOX

Diameter	3,643 km (2,264 miles)
Average distance from Jupiter	421,800 km (262,092 miles)
Diameter compared to Earth	0.29x
Mean surface temperature	–143ºC (–225ºF)
Did you know?	With over 400 active volcanoes, Io is the most geologically active object in the Solar System

EUROPA FACT BOX

meter	3,122 km (1,940 miles)
rage distance from Jupiter	671,100 km (417,002 miles)
meter compared to Earth	0.25x
an surface temperature	–190ºC (–310ºF)
you know?	Europa's surface is covered with up to 100km (62 miles) of ice, making it one of the smoothest and brightest objects in the Solar System

GANYMEDE FACT BOX

Diameter	5,262 km (3,270 miles)
Average distance from Jupiter	1,070,400 km (665,115 miles)
Diameter compared to Earth	0.41x
Mean surface temperature	–143ºC (–225ºF)
Did you know?	Ganymede is the largest satellite in the Solar System

Saturn

Our next stop is Saturn and we'll be there soon,

(As long as we don't crash right into that moon!).

You're certain to notice some fabulous things;

Fantastic and awesome Saturnian rings!

Billions of fragments of dust, rock and ice,

Suspended in Saturn's gravitational vice.

Like Jupiter, it's huge and made mostly from gas,

Though its centre is rocky – let's try not to crash!

He must do his job or you're food for a vulture;

Saturn was the Roman 'God of Agriculture'.

1,427 million km

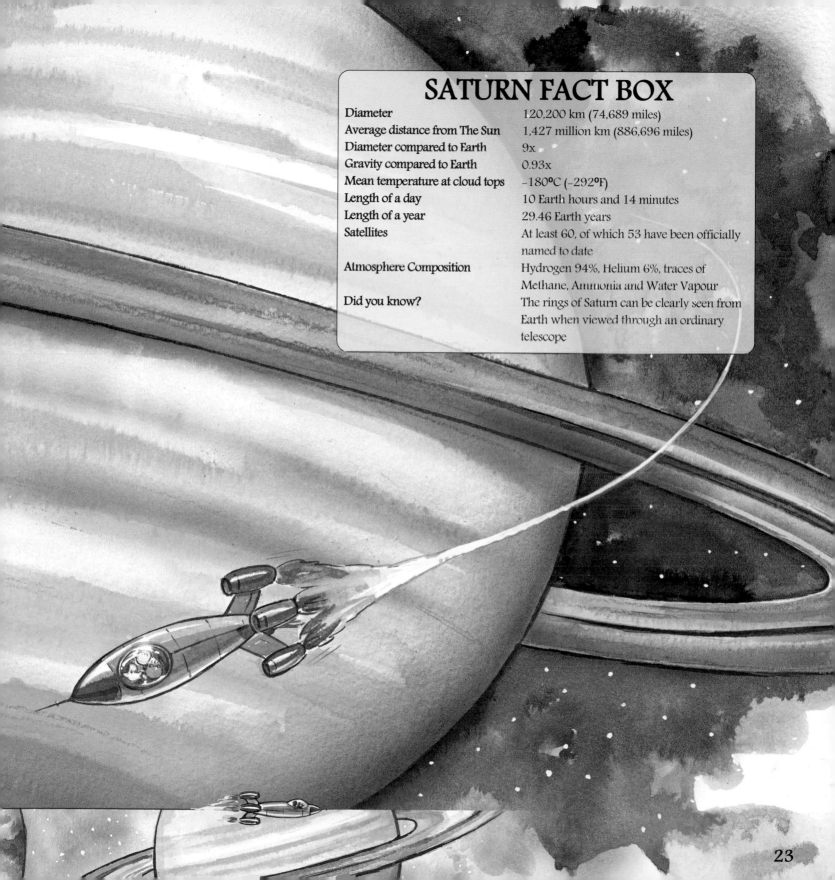

SATURN FACT BOX

Diameter	120,200 km (74,689 miles)
Average distance from The Sun	1,427 million km (886,696 miles)
Diameter compared to Earth	9x
Gravity compared to Earth	0.93x
Mean temperature at cloud tops	−180ºC (−292ºF)
Length of a day	10 Earth hours and 14 minutes
Length of a year	29.46 Earth years
Satellites	At least 60, of which 53 have been officially named to date
Atmosphere Composition	Hydrogen 94%, Helium 6%, traces of Methane, Ammonia and Water Vapour
Did you know?	The rings of Saturn can be clearly seen from Earth when viewed through an ordinary telescope

Saturn's Moons

What about moons? There are sixty of them

And one of those moons is the crème de la crème!

If moons were to worship a king of their own,

Then Titan would surely be sat on the throne!

The thing is you see – and I'm being sincere –

Titan's a moon with its own atmosphere.

But could life exist there? Is it too cold?

If you make your home there then you won't grow old!

TITAN FACT BOX

Diameter	5,150 km (3,200 miles)
Average distance from Saturn	1,221,870 km (759,235 miles)
Diameter compared to Earth	0.40x
Mean surface temperature	−180°C (−288°F)
Did you know?	Titan is the only moon in the Solar System that has an Earth-like atmosphere

1,427 million km

Enceladus is quite an interesting place,

It shoots plumes of water miles high into space.

Although it looks barren there may be a twist;

Because it has water then life might exist.

ENCELADUS FACT BOX

Diameter	500 km (310 miles)
Average distance from Saturn	238,000 km (147,886 miles)
Diameter compared to Earth	0.04x
Mean surface temperature	–201°C (–330°F)
Did you know?	Some scientists believe that, due to the existence of liquid water, Enceladus is the most likely place in the Solar System, apart from Earth, to support life

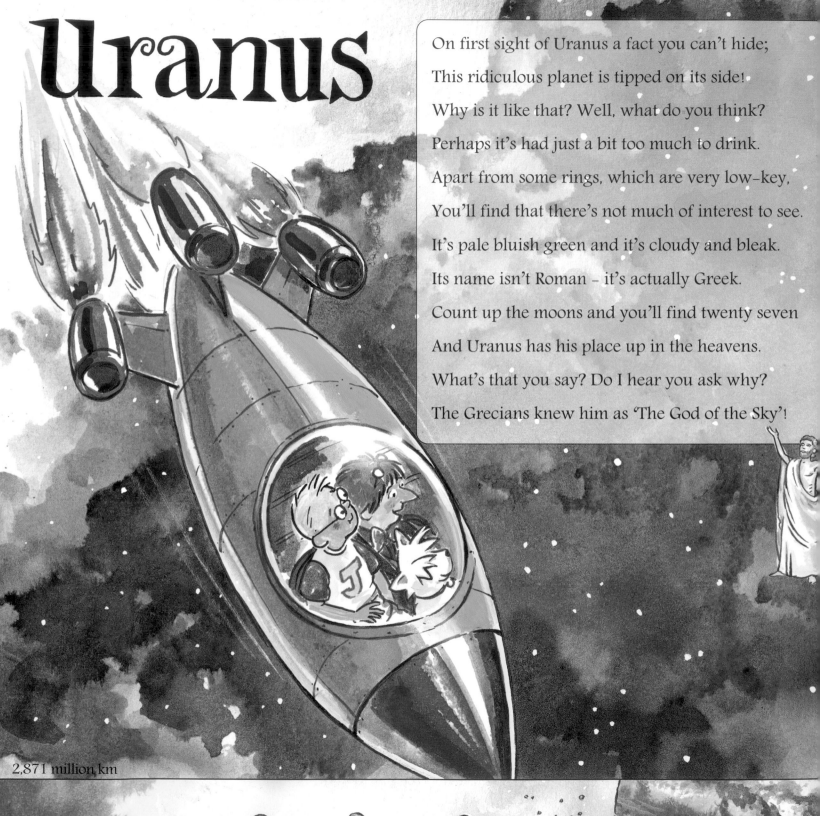

Uranus

On first sight of Uranus a fact you can't hide;

This ridiculous planet is tipped on its side!

Why is it like that? Well, what do you think?

Perhaps it's had just a bit too much to drink.

Apart from some rings, which are very low-key,

You'll find that there's not much of interest to see.

It's pale bluish green and it's cloudy and bleak.

Its name isn't Roman – it's actually Greek.

Count up the moons and you'll find twenty seven

And Uranus has his place up in the heavens.

What's that you say? Do I hear you ask why?

The Grecians knew him as 'The God of the Sky'!

2,871 million km

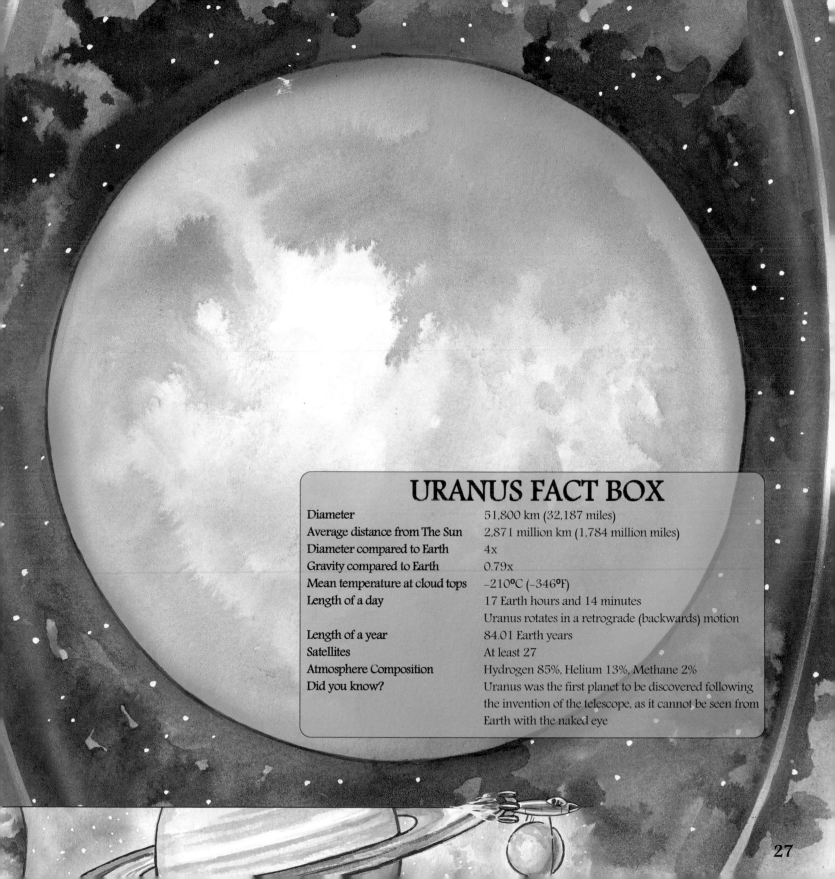

URANUS FACT BOX

Diameter	51,800 km (32,187 miles)
Average distance from The Sun	2,871 million km (1,784 million miles)
Diameter compared to Earth	4x
Gravity compared to Earth	0.79x
Mean temperature at cloud tops	−210°C (−346°F)
Length of a day	17 Earth hours and 14 minutes
	Uranus rotates in a retrograde (backwards) motion
Length of a year	84.01 Earth years
Satellites	At least 27
Atmosphere Composition	Hydrogen 85%, Helium 13%, Methane 2%
Did you know?	Uranus was the first planet to be discovered following the invention of the telescope, as it cannot be seen from Earth with the naked eye

Neptune

4,501 million km

Look out, there's Neptune, the mighty 'Blue Giant',

A planet that's not Health & Safety compliant!

Its liquids and gases have turned into ice –

We won't stick around long, an hour will suffice!

That's just long enough; we can count thirteen moons,

Then get going quick as there's icy monsoons!

Hey look, there's a storm; it's like Jupiter's 'Spot' –

But is it a red one? Not this time it's not!

There's no water here, but there should really be,

As the Romans named Neptune 'The God of the Sea'.

NEPTUNE FACT BOX

Diameter	49,528 km (30,775 miles)
Average distance from The Sun	4,501 million km (2,797 million miles)
Diameter compared to Earth	3.8x
Gravity compared to Earth	1.2x
Mean temperature at cloud tops	–220°C (–364°F)
Length of a day	16.11 Earth hours
Length of a year	164.80 Earth years
Satellites	At least 13, the largest of which, Triton, is geologically active
Atmosphere Composition	Hydrogen 85%, Helium 13%, Methane 2%
Did you know?	Neptune is the coldest 'true planet' in the Solar System

Halley's Comet

We're reaching the end of our interesting trip,

We'll make one last stop then we'll turn round the ship.

But hold on a minute, what's that up ahead?

Move out of its way or we'll find ourselves dead!

One of our engines is blowing a grommet,

What's blocking our path? It's Halley's Comet.

Comets are interesting things in my book,

Let's move a bit closer and have a good look.

As it flies through the heavens it loses its crust

And behind it, it leaves an immense trail of dust.

When nearing the Earth sunbeams light up these fumes

And we can enjoy its magnificent plumes.

But will it return? Yes, you should have no fears,

It visits the Earth every 76 years.

HALLEY'S COMET FACT BOX

Size	The nucleus of Halley's Comet is only c. 15 km (9.32 miles) long, c. 8 km (4.97 miles) wide and c. 8 km (4.97 miles) thick and is shaped like a peanut
Composition of the 'tail'	Water Vapour 80%, Carbon Monoxide 17%, Carbon Dioxide 3% with traces of Methane, Ammonia and dust
Last visible from Earth	1986 AD
Next visit to Earth	2061 AD
Did you know?	Halley's Comet appeared at the time of the Battle of Hastings in 1066 and was thought to have been a bad omen by the defeated British under King Harold II. It is visible from Earth on a cycle of 75 to 76 years.

Pluto (& Charon)

Our last stop is Pluto – it's distant and small!

Astronomers don't call it a planet at all,

But a celestial body that's known as a dwarf;

Do you think we might only be having a laugh?

Its cold, rocky surface is covered with ice;

I don't think we'll stop here, it isn't so nice!

Which Roman God could the great Pluto be?

I'll just do some research and then we will see.

Are you waiting patiently? Sat there agog?

He's 'The God of the Underworld'……and Mickey Mouse's dog!

5,913 million km

PLUTO FACT BOX

Diameter	2,320 km (1,441 miles)
Average distance from The Sun	5,913 million km (3,674 million miles)
Diameter compared to Earth	0.18x
Gravity compared to Earth	0.04x
Mean surface temperature	–230°C (–382°F)
Length of a day	6 Earth days and 9 hours
Length of a year	247.70 Earth years
Satellites	4, the largest of which, Charon, is over half the diameter of Pluto (1,210 km or 752 miles) and orbits around the same central point as Pluto, rather than around Pluto itself
Atmosphere Composition	It is believed that the atmosphere of Pluto consists mainly of Nitrogen, Methane and Carbon Dioxide
Did you know?	Pluto is smaller than seven moons in the Solar System – Earth's Moon, Ganymede, Callisto, Io and Europa (Jupiter), Titan (Saturn) and Triton (Neptune)

"*Thanks Daddy*," said Jacob, "*that really was great!*"

"No problem," laughed Patrick, "but it's getting late.

There's much more to tell you tomorrow," he said,

"But now I'm afraid it's time you were in bed!"

The Kuiper Belt

Although Patrick and Jacob have returned home, astronomers are discovering new worlds in an area of Space known as The Kuiper Belt. So far, several 'dwarf planets' have been identified and it is estimated that there may be 40 to 50 objects of comparable or greater size than Pluto (which itself is now deemed to orbit within the inner reaches of The Kuiper Belt).

Eris is the largest dwarf planet yet to be discovered.

Other dwarf planets which have been named are Haumea and Makemake.

Not much is known about objects in this region as it is simply too far away for our telescopes and explorative equipment to obtain all but the most rudimentary data.

4550 million km – 8250 million km

Pluto

Asteroid Belt

V

Sun

Mercury

Jupiter

Earth

Uranus

The Kuiper Belt

Neptune

Comet

Halley's Comet

Saturn

The Solar System

The Solar System

Sun

Mercury

Venus

Earth

Mars

Asteroid

Jupiter

Ceres

Saturn

Uranus

Neptune

Dwarf Planets

Pluto

Patrick & Jacob Suppor

Giving support to the families of sick children in hospital

It can be a frightening experience for children in hospital who have an injury or are seriously ill. Away from their normal, everyday life, it's important to have their closest family around.

Unfortunately for some children in hospital their parents aren't able to stay with them, and as so many hospitals are a long way from their homes, parents often spend time travelling that they would rather spend with their child.

"At The Sick Children's Trust, we believe that no child should be separated from their family while in hospital receiving treatment for a serious illness."

We provide free high-quality 'Home from Home' accommodation for the families of poorly children in hospital.

For sick children we can provide them with family love and support; for the family, we help reduce the emotional and financial worries of being away from home.

We have seven 'Homes from Home' at hospitals in the following cities: Cambridge, Leeds, London, Newcastle and Sheffield.

We would like to thank Kevin Price and all the readers of this book for supporting The Sick Children's Trust.

A child's experience

"When I came out of Intensive Care after my liver transplant my parents told me they were staying in a really nice 'Home from Home'. The day when I was able to go to the house I was really surprised - it was great and mum made me a lovely meal. My sister was able to stay too so we could all be together. Being with my family helped me to feel better quicker. I thank everyone at The Sick Children's Trust for playing a part in helping me to feel better - the house is a great place."

Matthew, aged 13, whose family stayed at Rainbow House at Great Ormond Street Hospital in London

Can you help us?

We rely completely on the generous donations of supporters to keep the families of seriously ill children together. It costs less than £30 to provide a room for a family for one night.

Fundraising at school

Does your school support any charities? Why not raise money for The Sick Children's Trust? You can have fun while you improve the lives of sick children at the same time.

For example, at school you could hold
- non-uniform days,
- cake sales,
- sponsored swims, reads or silences.

We would like to help

Contact us if you have any fundraising ideas or visit our website for more information about the work that we do and for fundraising suggestions and tips.

Donations

For information on how to make a donation please go to our website.

The Sick Children's Trust
3rd Floor, Willow House
17 - 23 Willow Place
London
SW1P 1JH

T: 020 7931 8695
E: info@sickchildrenstrust.org
www.sickchildrenstrust.org

we're here, so you can be there

Registered Charity No. 284416

45

The Silly Solar System – Glossary

Space Words

Asteroid – A lump of rock orbiting the Sun, smaller than a planet and most moons

Asteroid Belt – Region in space between Mars and Jupiter which contains millions of asteroids

Astronomer – Person who studies stars, moons, planets and anything in space

Atmosphere – A layer of gases surrounding a planet or star

Callisto – A moon orbiting Jupiter, one of the Galilean moons

Celestial – Of the Sky or Universe

Ceres – Dwarf planet found in the Asteroid Belt

Crater – A bowl shaped hole in the surface of a planet or moon caused by another object crashing into it

Earth – Third planet from the Sun

Enceladus – Small moon orbiting Saturn

Eris – Dwarf planet found in the Kuiper Belt

Europa – A moon orbiting Jupiter, one of the Galilean moons

Evening Star – Nickname for Venus when seen from Earth

Galileo –16th Century Italian astronomer (b. 1564, d. 1642)

Ganymede – A moon orbiting Jupiter, one of the Galilean moons and the largest moon in the Solar System

Gravity, Gravitational – A force that acts throughout the Universe possessed by any matter (material or substance). The larger the collection of matter (such as a planet or star), the more gravity it has

Halley's Comet – A small ball of rock and ice on a long orbit around the Sun which brings it close to Earth every 75 to 76 years.

Haumea – Dwarf planet found in the Kuiper Belt

Io – A moon orbiting Jupiter, one of the Galilean moons

Jupiter – Fifth planet from the Sun and the largest planet in our Solar System

Kuiper Belt – Region of space at the outer reaches of our Solar System containing many asteroid-like objects

Makemake – Dwarf planet found in the Kuiper Belt

Mars – Fourth planet from the Sun

Mercury – First planet from the Sun and the smallest true planet in the Solar System

Moon – A space object that orbits a planet

Neptune – Eighth planet from the Sun

Planet – A large, round object which orbits a star

Pluto – Dwarf planet found in the Kuiper Belt

Red Spot – Enormous storm visible on the surface of Jupiter (generally known as The Great Red Spot)

Satellite – An object trapped in another object's gravity, such as a moon

Saturn – Sixth planet from the Sun

Solar System – An area of space containing a star with planets orbiting around it

Space – The Universe beyond Earth's atmosphere

Star – An incredibly hot ball of gas in space, such as our Sun

Sun – The star at the heart of our Solar System

Telescope – An instrument used by astronomers to study objects in Space

Titan – Large moon orbiting Saturn. The only moon in our Solar System to have an Earth-like atmosphere

Uranus – Seventh planet from the Sun

Venus – Second planet from the Sun

The Silly Solar System – Index

Tricky Words

Acid – A liquid which can corrode metals in high concentrations

Agog – Eager, expectant

Agriculture – Growing of crops or rearing of animals

Awe – Admiration mixed with fear

Canal – Man-made waterway

Cloudlet – Small cloud

Crème de la crème – Another way of saying 'the best'

Freeze – Turn into ice or other solid through extreme cold

Fried – Cooked at extremely hot temperature

Frizzled – Cooked at extremely hot temperature until shrivelled up

Full Pelt – Another way of saying 'at top speed'

Fumes – Trails of vapour or gas

Girth – The distance around an object

Grecian – Person from Greece (also known as 'Greek')

Hostile – Unfriendly and inhospitable

Hue – Another word for 'colour'

Insane – Another word for 'mad'

Irregular – Varying, uneven

Monsoon – Very heavy downpour (on Earth, the Monsoon is a seasonal wind in Asia which brings periods of heavy rain)

Plume – A mass of gas, dust or liquid spread out in the shape of a feather

Poisonous – Harmful to humans and animals

Primordial Stew – A mixture of water, minerals and chemicals believed to be where life first formed on Earth

Ridiculous – Another word for 'silly'

Rudimentary – Not advanced or developed, basic

Rotating – Spinning around

Smithereens – Small fragments

Sphere – Ball shaped object

Suspended – (In this sense) held in place by gravity

The Victorians- People who lived in the reign of Queen Victoria (1837 – 1901)

Void – Empty space

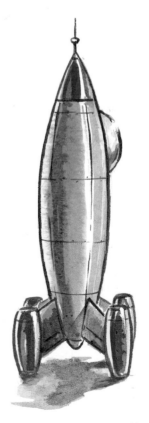

The End